BRICK BY BRICK
LADRILLO A LADRILLO

Heidi Woodward Sheffield
Traducido por Yanitzia Canetti

Nancy Paulsen Books

To Mom and Dad,
who built their lives
brick by brick

A Mamá y Papá,
que construyeron sus vidas
ladrillo a ladrillo

Nancy Paulsen Books
An imprint of Penguin Random House LLC, New York

Copyright © 2020 by Heidi Woodward Sheffield

Visit us online at penguinrandomhouse.com

Library of Congress Cataloging-in-Publication Data
Names: Sheffield, Heidi Woodward, author. | Title: Brick by brick / Heidi Woodward Sheffield.
Description: New York: Nancy Paulsen Books, [2020] | Summary: As a little boy watches his father,
a bricklayer, work hard to build the city, both dream of building a house of their own.
Identifiers: LCCN 2019018193 | ISBN 9780525517306 (hardcover: alk. paper) |
ISBN 9780525517320 (ebook) | ISBN 9780525517313 (ebook)
Subjects: | CYAC: Bricklaying—Fiction. | Fathers and sons—Fiction. |
Building—Fiction. | House construction—Fiction. | Hispanic Americans—Fiction.
Classification: LCC PZ7.1.S5114 Bri 2020 | DDC [E]—dc23
LC record available at https://lccn.loc.gov/2019018193
Manufactured in China by RR Donnelley Asia Printing Solutions Ltd.
ISBN 9780525517306
Special Markets ISBN: 9780593354667
Not for Resale
2 4 6 8 10 9 7 5 3

Design by Semadar Megged and Nicole Rheingans | Text set in Coventry ITC Std
The illustrations were created using photographs, digital painting, and collage.
Heidi used brick photos to create Papi and Luis, emphasizing their strength and fortitude.
Antique lace, embroidery, and textile images courtesy of The Lace Museum Detroit.
Image from *Design Motifs of Ancient Mexico* courtesy of Dover Publications, Inc.
Images from *361 Full-Color Allover Patterns* courtesy of Dover Publications, Inc.
Images from *Flowers* courtesy of Dover Publications, Inc.

This Imagination Library edition is published by Penguin Young Readers, a division
of Penguin Random House, exclusively for Dolly Parton's Imagination Library,
a not-for-profit program designed to inspire a love of reading and learning, sponsored
in part by The Dollywood Foundation. Penguin's trade editions of this work are
available wherever books are sold.

Mi papi es fuerte—
my papi is strong.

He's a bricklayer.
His arms are like stone.

Mi papi es fuerte:
my daddy is strong.

Él es albañil.
Sus brazos son como piedra.

When Papi builds,
he spreads the mortar thick.
TAP TAPS the brick in place.
SCRRRRAPES the drips.
Starts again.

Cuando Papi construye,
esparce el denso mortero.
TAP TAP el ladrillo en su lugar.
RRRASPA el mortero sobrante.
Y vuelve a empezar.

He helps build the city, brick by brick.

Ladrillo a ladrillo, ayuda a construir la ciudad.

At work, Papi climbs the scaffold
and touches the sky.
Papi is not afraid of heights.

En el trabajo, Papi sube al andamio
y toca el cielo.
En las alturas, no siente miedo.

Me neither.
At recess, I touch the sky, too.

Ni yo tampoco.
En el recreo, también el cielo yo toco.

Papi's work is
brick by brick.

El trabajo de Papi es
ladrillo a ladrillo.

Mine is
book by book.

El mío es
libro a libro.

all about
DOGS

I dream of a house for us.
Nuestra casa para siempre—
our always house—
with a garden for Mama
and maybe a dog for me.

Yo sueño con una casa para nosotros.
Our forever house:
nuestra casa para siempre,
con un jardín para Mamá
y tal vez un perrito para mí.

"When, Papi?"
"Someday," he says.

—¿Cuándo, Papi?
—Algún día —dice.

At lunch, Papi whistles,
eats Mama's special empanada,
drinks cinnamon horchata,
KERCHUNKS his lunch box closed.

En el almuerzo, Papi silba,
come la empanada especial de Mamá,
bebe una horchata de canela,
APLASTA y APLANA su lonchera.

I do, too.

Yo lo hago también.

Then it's back to work again.
Papi makes the mortar
that hold the bricks together.
He turns on the mixer,
WHIRRRRRRR,
pours the water,
WHOOSH.
He shovels sand and
adds cement.

Luego, regresa al trabajo.
Prepara el mortero
que mantiene unidos los ladrillos.
Enciende la mezcladora,
TURRRRRRRR,
vierte el agua,
GLU–GLU–GLU.
Palea arena y
agrega cemento.

I roll my clay,
SLAP and PAT.
I pinch and smooth
and mold it.

I make a tiny dog
and tiny bricks
for a tiny house.

Ruedo mi plastilina,
AMASO y APLASTO.
La aprieto, la aliso
y la moldeo.

Hago un perrito chiquitito
y unos ladrillos diminutos
para una casa pequeñita.

When the sunlight starts to fade,
dusty Papi picks me up.
He is tired, but smiling.

Papi feels like the sun,
hot and glistening.

Cuando la luz del sol
comienza a desvanecerse,
un Papi polvoriento
me recoge.
Está cansado,
pero sonriente.

Papi es como el sol,
cálido y resplandeciente.

Saturday is our special day.
Papi cooks me a yummy breakfast.
He lets me try his big hat on.

El sábado es nuestro día especial.
Papi me prepara un delicioso desayuno.
Deja que me pruebe su enorme casco.

"Close your eyes," Papi says. "Una sorpresa. A surprise."

—Cierra los ojos —dice Papi—. *A surprise*. Una sorpresa.

We ride away in his
rumbling truck.

The road is rough,
BUMP BUMP.
I want to sneak a peek,
but I don't.

Nos alejamos en su
ruidosa camioneta.

El camino tiene baches:
PUMP PUMP.
Quiero echar un vistazo,
pero no lo hago.

After a while, we stop.

Después de un rato, nos detenemos.

"¡SORPRESA!" Papi yells.

—SURPRISE! —grita Papi.

It's a new house
made of Papi's bricks!

¡Es una casa nueva
hecha con los ladrillos de Papi!

Tonight I dream
in my house.
Nuestra casa
para siempre—
our always house.

Esta noche sueño
en mi casa.
Our always house:
nuestra casa
para siempre.

And when spring comes,
I help Mama plant our flowers.

Y cuando llegue la primavera,
ayudaré a Mamá a plantar nuestras flores.